SUZANNAH ROWNTREE

The Rakshasa's Bride

First published by Bocfodder Press 2016

Copyright © 2016 by Suzannah Rowntree

All rights reserved. No part of this publication may be reproduced, stored or transmitted in any form or by any means, electronic, mechanical, photocopying, recording, scanning, or otherwise without written permission from the publisher. It is illegal to copy this book, post it to a website, or distribute it by any other means without permission.

This novel is entirely a work of fiction. The names, characters and incidents portrayed in it are the work of the author's imagination. Any resemblance to actual persons, living or dead, events or localities is entirely coincidental.

Second edition

Cover art by rebecacovers
Editing by Nadine Brandes Editorial

This book was professionally typeset on Reedsy. Find out more at reedsy.com

Chapter 1.

I n the village square, with the afternoon sun blazing whitely against dust and stone, Amma Madhu was singing again in a high keening wail.

"Oh Lord! Let none suffer the pains of love!"

Preeti hoisted the clay water-pot onto her head. Over in the inky pool of shade at the foot of the fort's wall, women squatted in a circle around Amma Madhu, who rose to her feet and moved to no beat save the wail of her own voice.

Her arms reached out and Preeti winced away, obscurely certain that the village midwife was pointing at her.

Brown arms twined with the sky.

"Love is a man of war, and kills everyone he touches!"

Preeti pulled the red pallu of her sari closer around her head, trying to shroud herself from view. Why did she think that coming to the well in mid-afternoon would save her from the distrustful eyes of these people, or from their whispers of the gods' curses and the evil eye? She should change her habits, come in the dawn with the crowd. Now, alone in the glaring white dust of the square, every window was an eye that pinned her down.

She adjusted the water-pot on her head and hurried across the square.

"Who can stand before him?" Amma Madhu keened. *"No one can resist Love!"*

Preeti ducked into a narrow alley between two houses that led to her father's hut. The sun vanished behind a cornice. It was as though she was struck suddenly blind, but she did not stop, mid-step, with a rattled gasp, because of that.

Someone had caught hold of her pallu.

The cloth pulled tight under the pot on her head and Preeti fought to keep it balanced, not daring to move. Her father was too poor now to afford another pot.

In the square, Amma Madhu cried, *"You may flee, but Love is a hunter, and nothing escapes his nets!"*

Even facing away from him, blind in the shadows, Preeti

knew it must be the young man who each afternoon watched her across the blazing square. It was the deep richness of his voice that was new to her. "Alone, hiding your face from view, you come out to the well when the sun is brightest." He circled into the range of her vision, still holding her prisoner with one bright filmy fold of cotton. "Why? What do you fear, lovely one?"

With a little gasp, Preeti dropped her gaze to the ground. She wanted to look at him, if she dared, once more to see him, fair-skinned, black-haired, clad in silk and linen with jewels smouldering on the silver hilt of his sword, but his very splendour struck fear into her. Why was he speaking to her, this young god? Why was he lying in wait for her?

The midwife's song threaded through her frantic thoughts. *"Oh Love! You have caught me, take pity!"*

Preeti kept her eyes on the ground, the column of her neck rigid beneath the water-pot. "My father is disgraced in business, lord. They say we have the evil eye."

His laugh was as slow and deep as his voice. "Impossible." His hand came under her chin and Preeti's eyes flicked up beseechingly. He smiled. "See?"

His lifted his other hand and passed it over her head, then clenched a fist and laid it against his temple.

"No," she murmured, and then bit her lip. It was only a gesture. Back in the happy days, her mother had done the same thing at her sister's wedding. But then her mother had died. And while her father's caravans were lost to storm and robbery, Radha's husband enjoyed unstinted success.

Not even Radha wanted anything to do with them now. Again, Preeti felt a dull ache of resentment. Mother had taken all Radha's bad luck. It was meant for her. Radha should have had it, not Preeti and their ageing father, not this young lord who glittered in the dark like a god and did not know what malice he had called down upon his head.

It was only a gesture.

He must have seen the worry in her eyes. His white teeth glinted. "You fear for me?"

"Yes, lord."

"Then I will give you a token so that you may not fear. My name."

"Bhagavan," she protested, dropping her eyes again and using the title she should give a lord who might be a god. Or if he wasn't a god? What honourable interest could a warrior like him take in her, a ruined merchant's daughter?

Over her protest he pulled her closer by the pallu. His breath tickled the strands of hair by her ear. Preeti scented oils and spices. If she'd only left the grain unmilled this morning, she might have gone down to the river, and washed away the dust and sweat; no matter if she no longer had unguents or spices to rub into her hair and body as she had in the happy years.

But if the smell bothered him, there was no sign of it in his voice.

"Remember that I, Sanjit, have broken your curse."

The pressure of the fabric against her head faded. The pallu drifted against her cheek. Preeti lifted her eyes and saw that she was alone in that narrow passage.

She turned and looked out into the brazen glare of the afternoon sun. She saw dozing dogs and ruminant cows. She saw the ring of men chewing betel over a game of Nava Kankari. She saw the circle of women around Amma Madhu. The midwife had fallen silent at last and stood with her arms at her sides, staring like a dog at point.

Preeti followed her gaze and saw the sun glint from the jewels on the scabbard of a tall splendid figure as he disappeared into the street that ran along the fort wall.

She resettled the water jar on her head and went on through the stifling dark toward her father's hut. Who *was* the lord Sanjit? Why did he shadow her steps? How could he say he had broken her curse?

It was a snare. She should keep her feet free of it; she had had enough of dishonour and heartbreak.

But when she came home, she found her father bundling his few possessions with trembling hands into a rolled mat. For while she lingered in the shadows with the Bhagavan, a message had come from Pradip Gupta the camel-driver, the master of one of his lost caravans.

"We'll be rich again," her father breathed into her hair as he hugged her good-bye.

For a moment Preeti allowed herself to imagine a future without bad luck, without whispers or pointed fingers or the cold silent fear of everyone hurrying by them with gazes averted, making the sign of the evil eye.

Maybe he *was* a god.

She pulled back, forcing her mind to the moment terrified to imagine such things. "Babuji, please. Just come back safely."

He smiled down at her through the beard that had gone white when her mother died at the time of the rains. "Tell me what I shall bring for you when I come home, Preeti."

She opened her mouth to ask for a bottle of sandalwood oil. Then closed it. Such presumption might very well earn her more grief. If their fortunes were restored, perhaps one day the gods would not laugh at her for spending money on luxuries. Until then, let her think of some gift better suited to her lot.

"All I want is a lotus flower." She reached down and touched his feet. "Pick me a red lotus flower on your way home, Babuji."

* * *

He did not return until the roads had already crumbled under the rains.

Preeti saw him coming from the roof of the hut, which she was attempting for the seventh futile time to patch, without skill or assistance. Since the Bhagavan Sanjit had stopped her in the alley on the day word came from Pradip Gupta, only Amma Madhu had gone out of her way to speak to her.

"Beware," the midwife had said at the well one morning. "You are marked down. Flee now."

Preeti had looked back into her eyes, wanting to flee indeed, but forced herself to ask:

"You saw him, the lord Sanjit?"

"I see more things than you imagine, damsel."

"Who is he?" Preeti pulled her dripping jar to the well's lip and held it before her like a shield. "Does he come from the fort?"

Amma Madhu lifted her eyes to the blind wall. "No one comes from the fort. It is empty."

"Why?"

"That song was forgotten long ago." She lowered her own jar to the water below, and the brass bangles on her arms crashed discordantly.

"There's a rajah, isn't there?"

Amma Madhu's eyes were veiled now. "Maybe." She lifted the pot to her head and was gone.

After that not even the midwife spoke to her. Therefore Preeti sat alone on the roof with a bundle of straw and tried to mend its leaks, until she heard hoofbeats, and looked up to see her father sitting a horse worth a prince's ransom, finer than anything she had seen in the city of her birth.

She slid from the roof and waited at the door with a tray of flowers and incense to welcome him.

He wouldn't meet her eyes as he pushed back his cloak—it was as splendid as the horse—and kissed her cheek over the tray of incense. Then, from under his cloak, he took out one perfect fire-red lotus flower.

"For you, Preeti," he said, and passed her into the house with a sigh as of great weariness.

She looked at his bowed shoulders under the fine cloak, and waited while the hope that had flooded into her at the sight of that horse drained away, drop by agonising drop.

"Babu?"

He pulled the cloak from his shoulders with quick, jerky motions. "Give me food first."

She made him sit and served him dahl. As she handed him the bowl, he glanced up from under his eyebrows. *He really is very worried,* she thought, in the moment before his voice cracked like a whip.

"Won't you have some?"

"There's not much left, Babuji."

"Let tomorrow see to itself. Eat, Preeti."

"There's—there's none left, Babuji. I saved this for you. In case you came home. Because I thought you might be hungry when you did."

"Folly!" He sprang to his feet. "Worthless child! What good are you to me, dead? Eat!"

"I—"

"Eat!" he roared, and wheeled around and went to the doorway. That magnificent horse was tethered there, staring at him with liquid eyes. Again her father's shoulders slumped, and his head dropped down, as if burdened by some dreadful secret.

Afterwards, Preeti found the lotus flower lying on the floor, where it had slipped from her numb and nerveless hand. She did not know when, but it must have been sometime in the long strangled silence that passed before she went to her father and put a hand on his shoulder. He half-turned to her with something that might have been a sob.

She had to clear her throat to speak past the lump of terror in her throat.

"Tell me, Babu."

* * *

Two years ago the name Om Nitin Kamla would have opened any door in the city of Cambay. To a merchantman of his standing, Brahmins and rajahs might almost defer without dishonour. For from him and his friends came the money for temples and armies and palaces, and to them came foreign rajahs and merchantmen eager to bring the wonders of the world—lions and peacocks, silks and stones, jewels and unguents for the gladdening of the hearts of every dweller in that bright-lit town, from the exquisite henna-painted gem-crusted ladies of the rajah's palace to the vivid street-birds who could not touch or own, but might see and be gladdened.

If Om Nitin Kamla had an equal in the world of trade it was Krisna Khan, to whom he married his elder daughter Radha—an alliance as brilliant as any made by a rajah for his kohl-eyed daughter. His younger daughter Preeti might have been a greater triumph. Om Nitin Kamla had kept his eyes open. He had taken her to all the right festivals, all the richest weddings. She deserved everything he could do for her, he argued.

And Shiva Malhotra was everything. Brahmin by birth, young, gentle, and just straitened enough in his fortunes to afford a tenderness for the merchant's lovely daughter.

An astrologer had already been consulted for an auspicious wedding date. But by the time the messenger returned with the lucky day, Om Nitin Kamla's wife was dead, his house had burned to the ground, and the first of his caravans was reported lost to bandits in the desert.

Shiva Malhotra reconsidered. Krisna Khan became suddenly very busy. Even Radha pretended she didn't know them. And Om Nitin Kamla and Preeti went north, fleeing their bad luck, to the little village of the merchant's birth where they might live quietly with a milch cow and a garden.

He'd dreaded ever returning to the scene of his fall. Only Pradip Gupta's triumphant return could have lured him from hiding. And yet if doors opened for him in the city now, they opened only on debts and creditors. In the end, Om Nitin Kamla left the city richer than he had gone only by ten silver coins.

He put them into the pouch he wore against his skin, saddled his donkey, and began his long ride home. The only consolation that came to him, like a shaft of light through the clouds of his gloom, was the thought that he could at least afford Preeti's gift.

The rains, blinding and lashing, came late one afternoon while he plodded down a tree-shadowed path above the river. He should have stopped and taken shelter until the storm passed, but he was tired and too disheartened to care for his safety. Instead he pressed on, leading his donkey on foot and feeling for the path ahead of him with the end of his staff like a blind beggar.

The whole world was a roar of wind and falling rain. Thus he did not hear the floodwater until it charged upon him like a stampede of cattle.

When he came to himself, he was bruised, beaten and cold. One arm was caught in the iron bars of a gate. Water lapped at his bare feet: his shoes had been stripped away. He coughed up water and rose, clawing at the gate.

It opened.

Om Nitin Kamla spat up a little more water and looked again. He saw a garden, felt a soft warm breeze blowing, and looked up further to see a magnificent palace lit by the moon.

Outside the gate, water grumbled at his feet and dripped from the trees.

The merchant stumbled up the gravel road toward the palace, rasping in a painful breath with each step. With his bad luck, the guards of this place would throw him back into the river the moment they saw him.

But he encountered no guards.

The door of the palace opened at a touch. He went in light-headed from weariness, and found himself in a white courtyard surrounded by arched doorways with blowing white curtains. In the middle of the courtyard, like gems set in silver, were five pools in the shape of a flower. They were covered with buds, red and pink and snowy white.

Lotuses.

Om Nitin Kamla limped to the water. The night breeze was fragrant with the flowers' breath. He inhaled the scent for a moment. Preeti's gift?

Perhaps he could take one home with him.

Perhaps he would live to go home.

He went up the stairs toward the door opposite the one he had come in by. Here the white curtain was looped back on a silver hook and he went inside to find a little burning brazier and a tray bearing bread and a bowl of meat beside a curtained couch wrought in silver.

He looked around. There was no one here to slam doors in his face, as they had in the city. Perhaps, presently, one would come and turn him out. Until then…

He didn't mean to eat all of it. But the meat was so tender, the bread so oily and crisp, that he had wiped the bowl clean, dabbed up the last of the crumbs on his fingertips, and pitched wearily into the couch cushions almost before he realised what he had done.

Let them turn him out if they wished. Until then he would sleep.

* * *

When Om Nitin Kamla awoke, the sun had risen high enough to fill the whole room with light. For a little while he lay on the couch, lost in the flashing colours and the mind-mazing patterns that adorned the walls. Then suddenly he remembered where he was, and started up.

All the aches had vanished from his body. He felt—not merely well, but five years younger. Let them turn him out now, and he would walk home whistling. He rubbed sleep out of his eyes, glanced at the tray beside the couch—and caught his breath.

The wiped-clean dishes of the night before had gone. In their place was dahl and stuffed paratha, as fragrant and tempting as any he had eaten in the palaces of Hyderabad or Lahore. On the floor, a pair of stout shoes. Beside them, neatly folded, a gorgeously-embroidered cloak which as a matter of habit his mind appraised, priced, and marvelled at.

Not only would he not be turned out, but he would be left to sleep in peace, and then fed and clothed like a prince.

He ate the food, pulled on the shoes, and then went out into the courtyard. A flutter of movement caught his eye... Only the white curtains. No other motion or sound disturbed the peace of that place.

The lotus-flowers were like white and red fire on the pond's breast.

Om Nitin Kamla called out. There was no answer and the shattered silence was so dreadful that he could not find the courage to break it again. Instead he crept to one of the other doorways and peeked behind the white curtain. He saw another room, more splendid than the first, yet just as empty. The next was like it.

The whole place stood lifeless.

He looked into the sky. It was a fine day; he should make the most of the weather, and start for home. He had no food and he had lost everything except his ten silver coins. But his stomach was satisfied and his bruises had healed. He felt a little more bold, so he went back into his room and put on the embroidered cloak. Then he descended the steps to the pools. The lotus-flowers clustered just beyond his reach, almost as if they meant to avoid him, but at last he stretched far enough to close his hand around a stem and jerk.

At the moment that the passionate red flower came away in his hand, he felt a hot breath on the back of his neck, felt blazing eyes boring into his skull, and turned with a cry of terror.

The creature stood looming over him, a nightmare beast walking manlike on its hinder legs; fanged, clawed, maned, with black fur and eyes of fire, as if a temple carving had come to horrible life.

A Rakshasa.

So the stories were true.

Om Nitin Kamla tried to scramble backward, but the

Rakshasa hooked its claws into his tunic and yanked him level with its scowling face.

"Who told you you might pick my lotus?"

"Sir—lord—"

"I welcome you to my house. I feed you and clothe you. I give you every comfort and tranquillity. Is this how you repay me?"

"Your generosity," said Om Nitin Kamla feebly, "is truly beyond all mortal comprehension—. I came to believe you would not grudge so small a thing as a lo—"

"Small?" the Rakshasa roared. "Small?" He shook Om Nitin Kamla like a rat. "Is a thief any less a thief if the thing he takes is small? Is he any less deserving of punishment?"

Om Nitin Kamla abandoned any hope in finesse. When the creature released him, he crumpled onto his face. "Have mercy, lord! My luck has already broken me and indeed, I would be better dead already if it were not for my daughter, the delight of my eyes and the only remaining staff of my age. I offered her anything money could buy. A lotus-flower was all she would ask of me."

The Rakshasa stepped back, and the fire of his eyes seemed less terrible. But his voice, when he spoke, was a low forbidding rumble. "And you lay your guilt upon this daughter of yours, this delight of your eyes."

Om Nitin Kamla did not dare to look up. But he fumbled at his waist, and drew out the ten silver coins in his pouch. "Take it," he begged. "It is all that is left of Om Nitin Kamla, once the richest man in Gujarat. Take it, that I may go back to my daughter and starve with her for as long as the gods desire in this birth to punish us."

"Your daughter need not starve," said the Rakshasa.

Om Nitin Kamla raised his face. The creature crouched over him like a clenched fist above a gnat, and he could see venom dripping from its yellow tusks.

"I will let you go free on one condition. Give your daughter to me."

Preeti, for whom the Brahmin Malhotra had proven himself unworthy? Given to this monster? Om Nitin Kamla gave a despairing cry.

The Rakshasa did not seem to hear him. "Let her come of her own will, and save your life, if she has the courage, and if she loves you so much. If she does not, then return to me. And do not seek to avoid your fate, for know that my vengeance will find you both, Om Nitin Kamla. Are we agreed?"

His only answer was a sob.

"*Are we agreed?*" the Rakshasa roared, and Om Nitin Kamla would have done anything—*anything*—to escape.

"Yes! Yes!" he cried.

"That is well for you." The Rakshasa withdrew and pointed to the door. "A horse is waiting outside to take you home. When you are ready to return, with your daughter or alone, mount the horse and he will know where to bring you." The monster made as if to turn, and paused. "Where is your home?"

"The village is named Arora."

"A rebellious people." The Rakshasa glowered. "Treacherous in every generation, yielding neither due service nor just tribute. In good time I will return to that place and exact every last copper. Every last soul." He stretched out a clawed hand and pointed to the pavement. "In the meantime, your silver is accepted against that debt. Leave it on the stones."

The tears rolled down the face of Om Nitin Kamla, but he did not dare to disobey. He laid the coins on the floor in two forlorn little piles, bowed to the Rakshasa's retreating back, and left.

* * *

Preeti did not look at her father. She sat slumped against the wall in the hut with her fingers pressed against her mouth, looking at the abandoned bowl of dahl on the floor and, next to it in the dust, the red flower that had cost so much.

Her father stood leaning against the door, still staring out. At last he stirred and turned back to her. "I'm sorry. For coming back. I should have stayed and—"

Preeti's breath whispered against her fingers. "Babu, no—"

"Before I return to him," he said, "I'll sell the cloak. You can use the money to live on until the harvest."

She rose from the floor and picked the lotus flower up out of the dirt. "No, Babu, I'm glad you came back. This is all my fault. I asked for the flower. I'll go to the Rakshasa.

"You don't know what you're saying. You haven't seen him."

"That makes it easier for me to do what I must."

"Preeti, no."

"I am the one who brought this bad luck on you, Babuji."

"I can't let you—

"Why not?" Preeti forced a smile. "It would be cruel of you to go away and leave me all alone."

"At least you would live."

"He didn't say he meant to kill me."

"No, but—"

"Please." She seized his hands and looked into his face, willing him to see how important this was to her. "Please. Let me do this. *My* fault. *My* bad luck. No one else will suffer for me."

Her father didn't answer. Only, with tears streaking his face, he lifted his hand to stroke her hair, and she knew she had carried her point.

When she fell asleep at last, sometime after midnight, Preeti dreamed that she went into the village square to draw water while the rain fell in sheets around her like the seas of an invisible shipwrecked world in the sky.

Her drenched sari pulled tight. She stopped, but did not turn around.

His voice was as warm as a lover's embrace. "Where are you going, O lovely one?"

"Let me go. I must draw water."

"There is no need for that, surely."

She glanced down at her pot. It was brimming full, pockmarked and stormy under the hammer-blows of raindrops it could not hold.

Preeti turned. "Bhagavan?"

But no one was there.

She awoke and lay staring into the dark. It was difficult to sleep with the ache of hunger in her belly. At first light she put on the worthless tin earrings and nose-ring that alone remained from her jewel-chest, draped her sari, faded and dirty as it was, with painstaking care, and went out to the well.

Amma Madhu squatted there as usual, speaking to two friends as they waited for the crowd around the well to thin a little. Preeti went directly up to her, pressed her two palms together, and murmured, "Namaste."

She hardly spoke loudly enough to be heard. But the chaffer stopped as if she had bitten them.

Amma Madhu looked up at her with a regal air, as if she were the queen of this corner of the village. "Namaste."

"Please," said Preeti, "if you know, tell me where to find the Bhagavan Sanjit."

Shocked silence, nudgings, whisperings. Preeti's cheeks warmed. But she knew what she risked by such a question. Amma Madhu stared back at her impassively and at last jerked her head south, toward the trees.

"You are going to the Demon Rajah, *naheen?*"

Preeti's fingers whitened on the water-jar. "How do you

know?"

"I see many things." Amma Madhu shrugged. "Many brides that one has taken. One in every generation."

"What became of them?"

"Ashes."

"He killed them?"

Amma Madhu tilted an eyebrow and looked at her for a while, as if determining whether to tell the truth. At last she nodded, once, and grunted. "Yes."

Preeti swallowed hard and drew a breath. But Amma Madhu spoke again before she could say a word.

"Do not hope that the Bhagavan Sanjit will aid you. That flirt! Always an eye for a pretty girl. Where he comes from, none of us knows. Where he goes to, none of us knows. He makes sweet promises, and stirs up foolish hopes, and vanishes at the first sign of trouble. But the Rakshasa does everything he promises. *Everything.*"

Preeti backed away from Amma Madhu, trembling.

"Go to the Demon Rajah." The midwife's eyes were hard as flint. "Go! Buy us peace a little longer!"

Preeti turned to escape, but she had run only a few steps when she saw him.

The Bhagavan.

He sat a horse in the mouth of the street that ran by the fort, his jewelled accoutrements flashing and flaring in the dim clouded light. For a moment, their eyes met, and then he turned his horse toward her, touching his heels to its flanks. But Preeti turned her back on him and fled down the narrow passage that led to her father's hut.

It was too good to be true. He could not really break her curse.

She could not bear to draw out her misery any longer. That evening she made a little bundle of her spare sari, mounted the Rakshasa's horse behind her father, and set off for the Rakshasa's palace.

* * *

The horse seemed to fly rather than gallop. Preeti shut her eyes dizzily at the speed and clasped her arms more tightly around her father's waist. But how foolish to be frightened by a fast horse when she knew not what terror awaited her in the house of the Rakshasa!

And the lord Sanjit vowed her bad luck was over!

Amma Madhu was right about him, of course; from the first, her instincts had warned her away from him. Poor, she could be nothing but a flirtation to him. But if things were different? If they were rich again?

The horse slackened its pace, bringing her back to the hard present, and she heard her father say, "Look, Preeti."

Through the iron gate that stood open before them a gravel path ran up through pools and trees and flowering shrubs to a tall white palace whose front was a fretwork of pillars and windows. A flight of steps ran up to the entrance, a pillared white portico with pale-yellow birds and flowers etched in the frieze.

Somewhere, a peacock screamed. At the same moment, there was a loud *crack* and one blazing fire flower broke across the sky in the shape of a red lotus.

The sparks did not fall or fade but hung for a long time burning in the sky as Om Nitin Kamla and his daughter went up the path to the stair and dismounted. In that light, the whole palace flushed pink.

For a while they stood hand in hand on the steps. A faint music rippled through one of the windows, and Preeti looked up at her father mournfully. "The Rakshasa must be hungry, to make such a rejoicing."

Om Nitin Kamla pulled back. "Preeti, there is still time. Ride home while you can."

"It's me he wants, not you, Babuji." Preeti thought of the brides Amma Madhu had spoken of. "And he knows I am here now. It is too late for me to flee, even if I wished to."

"O my delight!" said the merchant, sighing. "Let us bid one another farewell now. Before It comes."

Preeti nodded, drew her pallu a little more tightly around her head, and reached down to touch his feet. But for the first time, her father stooped quickly and caught her by the shoulders halfway.

"No." Instead he folded her into his embrace.

At last they took hands again and went on through the portico to the courtyard beyond.

Set into the white flags of the floor were five pools in the shape of a flower with candles burning on the brink. There were the lotus-flowers of which she had heard. More light shone from every doorway, gilding the flowers and the small potted trees that guarded the place with a yellow and welcoming glow.

In that light it was strange and almost frightening that the only sound to be heard was the wind billowing the white door-curtains and the strains of sad music going on and on just on the border of hearing. The fitful breeze came and went, sometimes revealing and sometimes concealing the sound, but then the breeze died away long enough for Preeti to recognise Amma Madhu's song.

The hair prickled on her scalp, and she tugged at her father's elbow, but he had gone still as stone and nearly as cold. Preeti followed his gaze to the doorway opposite. A shadow blocked the light. Her heart jolted. They stood in the presence of the Rakshasa.

She stood hand-in-hand with her father for the space of five thundering heartbeats. Then she went on, pulling Om Nitin Kamla behind her. Down the steps, across the courtyard, around the lotus-pool, pausing finally at the foot of the steps where the Rakshasa waited.

Because he stood with his back to the light, all she saw was a gigantic black silhouette, and a red gleam, as of smouldering eyes.

She might be wearing worthless tin and a sari of cheap red cotton, but Preeti Kamla had once been a welcome guest in houses nearly as splendid as this one. Stifling all her terror was the sudden desperate need to pretend she was not afraid of him. She pressed her two work-worn palms together and bowed with slow deliberate grace.

Beside her, more hastily, her father did the same.

The Rakshasa spoke in a low growling rumble that vibrated in her lungs and nearly shredded her thin calm. "You have kept your oath, Om Nitin Kamla. I am well pleased. My servants are loading your horse with treasure."

Her father bowed again. Preeti stole a glance at him and realised that he was too terrified to speak. Her own panic caught her by the throat—

The Rakshasa said her name. "Preeti Kamla, do you come willingly? Are you prepared to stay here?"

"Yes," she breathed, keeping her head bent.

"That is well."

Preeti stole another glance at her father. *Go,* her eyes told him. He fell back a step, as if her look had for a moment broken the immense exercise of willpower that held him by her side.

Had she not made up her mind to die, she might also have found it hard to stand there in candlelight and shadows before the Rakshasa.

"Yes, go," said the monster unexpectedly. "Say farewell to your daughter, merchant."

But Om Nitin Kamla backed away from her with a face blank with terror. No wonder he had insisted on saying goodbye outside, in the portico.

She gave a smile, and lifted her hand in farewell. There was an answering tremor of grief and tenderness under his beard. Then he turned and fled. After a little moment there was no sound but the drum of his horse's hoofs.

Preeti stood looking after him. The courtyard was very beautiful in moonlight and candlelight, and while she stood with her back turned on the Rakshasa she could almost imagine that she was alone.

Maybe he would kill her now. Now, with her back turned, and the image of her father still in her eyes, so that she could die on a memory of love.

He did not. She heard nothing but the plaintive wail of Amma Madhu's song. At last she stole a glance over her shoulder to see if he was still there.

He was. Waiting. He had all the time in the world to play with her, if he wished. Bride? Meal? Sacrifice? Which was she?

In the thread of a voice she asked, "What are you going to do with me?"

His answer was to set a clawed foot forward. Then another. Preeti backed as he came down the white stair to loom over her in the courtyard. The soft light of moon and candles fell on him and for the first time she really saw him: saw the curving yellow fangs, the mane black as pitch, the scowling face and the stripes of red above the eyes. He was something like a bear, something like a lion, and something like a black flame. Also he smelled of something half-sweet and entirely foul.

Preeti backed until her heel knocked against one of the candles by the side of the lotus pools. It rolled a short way and went out. The Rakshasa halted in his advance, clear in all his grim splendour under the light of the moon, and stretched out one taloned paw.

"Marry me, Preeti Kamla."

She drew in a breath that turned to ice and splintered in her throat. She swallowed the cold shards with a little whimper and pressed the back of her hand to her mouth to stifle her scream.

"Well?" His voice was implacable.

"I will obey my lord in everything." Her cheeks were wet. She realised that she had been crying with terror for a little while now.

"You do not understand me." He must be angry with her now, if he had not been before. "I do not command. I ask. Of your own heart give assent, or not at all."

She stole a glance at him. Marry that demon? Unbidden, the laughing face of the handsome warrior in the village rose up before her eyes and she felt an irrational dreary assurance that if she had gone to him, if she had begged for help, things would have been different tonight.

Maybe he would yet seek her. Maybe he would follow her. Maybe he would find her, even here.

She ducked her head. "Don't be angry with me, lord."

"I am not angry," he said in the same growl. "Come. I will show you to your room."

Chapter 2.

Preeti awoke to light, the sound of birdsong, and the far-off chimes of wind bells. At once she pushed herself to her elbow and looked around the room.

It was pillared and painted in gold and white, hung with golden tassels about the walls and flooded with light from scalloped windows. Splendid, and silent, and very lonely.

She pulled aside transparent white curtains and slid out from between the cushions and bolsters to explore the rest of it.

Breakfast was provided. She ate only a few mouthfuls for the rich bread and meat sat heavily in her stomach. In the centre of the floor, at the end of a long shallow stair a pool of water waited with marigold flowers lining its margin. Last night she had been too tired and too terrified to do anything but cry herself to sleep. This morning after a nervous glance into the empty passage beyond the curtains of her door, she untucked her sari, peeled off choli and petticoat, and dipped her foot into the water.

Heat. Her foot disturbed a coil of steam, bearing with it some subtle fragrance. She went down the seven steps and sank below the surface.

When she came out of the bath, she saw with a little scared shiver that her bundle of old, dirty clothes, carried with such care from the village last night, had vanished. In their stead a new sari lay folded on the bath's brink. By it stood a chest full of jewellery, and beyond that a great number of bottles and jars and bowls holding cosmetics: all the paraphernalia of beauty from the old happy days.

First she rubbed herself with oil and put on the fresh new choli and petticoat provided, the former stiffly bordered with golden coils and beads. Next she kohled her eyes. Then she dipped her finger into the sindoor, and made one practised dab with her forefinger between her eyebrows. Mehndi had been provided, and she carefully painted suns on the palms of her hands and the tops of her feet. When this had dried, she combed her hair and then dabbed perfume on earlobes, hands, and feet.

After this she draped her sari and fastened it in place with new brass pins. Then followed the jewellery. Two stacks of glass and gold bangles for each arm. Earrings and a pendant for her forehead. A nose ring, two necklaces, and rings for each finger. Finally, two golden anklets with chiming bells.

Golden anklets? Preeti dropped them as if they had burned her. No one wore gold on their feet, of course, so as not to insult the goddess Lakshmi, to whom it was sacred. For a moment she almost made up her mind not to wear them. Apart from her fear of the goddess, she did not want to walk with chiming steps through this enormous, echoing place.

Yet in the end she put them on. If the Rakshasa had provided the anklets, he must mean her to wear them, and she was more afraid of his displeasure than of the goddess Lakshmi's.

She must have been hours getting ready. Just as she took a step toward the door, a tiny rattle sounded behind her and she whisked around. She saw nothing, except that the cosmetics and the jewel-boxes and the cloth on which she had dried herself had all been cleared away.

She almost fled out her door into the palace, only to find herself in a long corridor lit by round white lamps hanging from domed ceilings. Patterns of birds and flowers twined across every surface. There was a dado along the wall at waist height, beneath which orange-trees and cypresses were painted, and above them sprawled magnificent country landscapes full of figures hunting and playing and listening to music.

Her bare feet sank into the carpet. *Chink, chink,* said her anklets.

She had to find the Rakshasa. She had to make him finish what he had started. She had to find him wherever he was hiding in this palace that seemed so full of watching eyes. Every so often the constant jingling babble of her feet wore her nerves thin and she rose up on tiptoe to hear the whispers of sound that dragged at her hearing under the laughter of bells.

Yet however long she stood listening, nothing came to break the silence, and she went on under the endless red-and-blue domes and arches. At last she turned a corner onto a cloistered balcony where the sun lay in pools on tiles frantic with colour, and clapped a hand to her mouth, for she saw what she thought to be a dwarf in a grey coat walking away from her on spindly legs. The next instant she recognised it as a heron, and drew a rattled breath. It went on ahead of her like a guide, and presently passed by a monkey with a little black face sitting on the baluster. The heron led her into an open room at a corner of that labyrinthine place, where she found a hundred other birds coming and going through the windows in a storm of song.

Beyond that she found a room of musical instruments, and for a while made herself sit and pick out old songs on the sitar. But the pluckings of her fingers only made the silence of the place more alarming. She laid the instrument down and went on, wandering through rooms filled with chairs and rooms filled with books—useless to her since no one had ever taught her to read—through rooms filled with flowers and trees, through rooms covered with beaten gold, and through rooms that had nothing at all in them but vast shimmering floors.

The sun fell behind the horizon at the same moment that Preeti pushed back a curtain and went through another doorway and found the Rakshasa.

From his posture, facing her with his claws clasped behind his back, she guessed he had heard the chime of her footsteps and was expecting her. She had just about given up expecting him at all, and at the sight of him, she fell back a step with a sudden numb sensation of mortality.

He held out a beckoning claw. "Let me see you."

She came forward as far as she dared, which left perhaps ten paces between them, and stared at his black-haired feet which, like a bird's, had one talon stretching back and three forward.

"You know what you are about," he said, and then, "Come and eat."

For the first time she saw where a meal was laid out on a low table. The Rakshasa settled himself cross-legged on a gem-scattered throne. Through the arched doorways leading to the garden, Preeti heard more music and the sound of running water.

Mingled with the scent of flowers and a mild warm

night, she breathed in spices, fruit, jasmine rice...

"Come and eat." The fear the monster's voice put into her flogged her forward a step before she looked at his face again.

To reach the food, she would need to halve the distance between them. Her stomach moved longingly. She stood undecided.

"Are you not hungry?" the Rakshasa asked her.

"Yes, lord."

"Then come. There is more than enough."

"Let my lord eat first. I will wait."

He shook his head. "I have other fare. I have come to see you eat."

Other fare.

Chink. Chink. Preeti forced herself forward and sank to her knees at a corner of the table as far away from the Rakshasa as she could manage. She took only the food she could reach, and crumbled a little into her mouth.

"Is all to your liking?" the Rakshasa asked suddenly.

She dared not look up, so she bent her head a little in acknowledgement. "Yes, lord."

"You are free of the whole house. And all the gardens. I ask only that you not go beyond the wall."

His words were kind, and even his voice sounded less forbidding than she remembered. "My thanks, lord."

Her hunger was satisfied. She sat with her hands on her knees, and the silence stretched out while she stole glances at the Rakshasa's teeth, so brutally apt for stripping meat rom bones, and wondered if she should starve herself for ear of what might happen if she became fat.

He was going to eat her, wasn't he?

She clenched her fists. "What do you mean to do with me?"

He did not answer and at last she realised he was waiting for her to look him in the eye.

"Marry me, Preeti."

Her mouth went dry. "Please, no. No."

His head inclined, and then with a heave like a mountain falling, he rose from his throne.

"Then I will bid you farewell for tonight."

And leave her alone in this horrible beautiful place, with its voiceless presences and twisting corridors! Preeti jumped to her feet. "I am lost. I don't know my way back to my room."

"Look for it when you want it."

The Rakshasa went out by an arch in the wall. After the curtain fell behind him, Preeti could not hear a whisper of sound, not a foot-fall. She stood in the room for a little longer, stretching her ears, imagining him lying in wait for her there until she could stand it no longer. With a peal of bells and bangles, she ran to the curtain and whisked it aside.

White lamps, like moons, stretched away down an endless ornamented corridor. The Rakshasa had gone.

* * *

Preeti was not sleepy, so she went back to the music room (how she found it, she did not know, except that she went looking for it, and discovered it up a stair and inside the first door she tried), took the sitar, and went outside into the garden. The sound of falling water led her to a pavilion with curtained arches on a pavement by a pool with a high tumbling waterfall. Here her playing and singing would not jangle as it had against the stark silence of the palace.

She began to sing, softly at first.

"He who walks in the shadow of love will have heaven beneath his feet. Come, beloved..."

And then she heard it, and with a wild jangle the sitar fell silent, but the voice went on singing out of the shadows under the trees.

"Come, beloved, and learn of love. Who can resist love? Who can turn his back on the brightness of heaven?"

He came out into the moonlight and Preeti caught her breath. It was the lord Sanjit.

"Just look at your madman, beloved! I search for you in the garden of heaven."

Preeti laid the sitar aside and rose and went toward him.

"Come, beloved, walk in heaven and learn of love." He caught her hand from her side and kissed it. It was a courtly gesture, but she had never seen it before, and she snatched her hand back with a little gasp. He smiled at her and went on singing. *"Walk in heaven, walk in the shadow of love."* To her horror, he snatched off one of the long swinging gold earrings hooked over her ears, and sent it

34

spinning off into the pool of water. Then—so dextrously that she barely felt it—he plucked out her nose-ring and sent it tumbling after.

"No!" Preeti tried to catch his quick hands, but he moved faster than she did, and caught both of her wrists in one hand and reached for her other earring with the other.

He was laughing at her. "Hold still, sweetheart. I want to see the real Preeti, not this mask of gold."

"No," she cried again. "The Rakshasa gave me these. If I lose them—"

"Tell him they were stolen." The Bhagavan captured her other earring. But he did not throw it into the water.

"Tell him?" Preeti wailed. "If he knows you have come, he will kill both of us... Oh, I am the unluckiest girl alive."

She broke into tears and the laughter faded from the lord Sanjit's face. Suddenly there was a splash as he followed her jewellery into the pool. Preeti stared at the rippling water in frozen surprise for the space of three breaths before his dark head broke the surface. He came back to her streaming water, and put the nose-ring and both earrings into her hand.

"Have you forgotten? I told you not to fear. I have taken your bad luck upon myself."

She gripped his hands with the jewels between them. "Why? Why? What help is that to me? I must have sinned in a previous birth. Anything I do not suffer for in this birth must be suffered for in another. Everyone understands this. Everyone is content to leave us to our punishment. Why not you?"

"Because you were made for love, Preeti."

She could only stare at him, motionless, silent, with what seemed a wild bird fluttering inside the cage of her ribs.

"The punishment was never meant for you to bear alone. It was never meant for you to bear at all. It was meant for me." He smiled, folding the jewels into her hands, then lifting them again to kiss them. "Your punishment is on my head now."

"Is it?" If only she could believe. "Is it? I am trapped here and the Rakshasa is going to marry me and maybe eat me as well—"

He caught her temples in his hands and stroked her tears away with his thumbs. "Shh. *Bus.* Trust me, Preeti."

She blinked, trying to stem the flow. "Please help me. Please take me away from this place."

He hesitated.

She shrugged away from him with a little hopeless sigh. "Oh, it's useless, I know. He will only hunt me down, and both of us will die for it."

"Don't trust to appearances, Preeti."

"Appearances?" She sniffed and backed a step. Suddenly all the old questions came back to her. "Who are you, anyway? Where do you come from? Who are you that you can take my bad luck?"

"Who am I?" A sad smile. "If I were to tell you, Preeti,

you would not be able to bear it."

A horrible suspicion crossed her mind and she stumbled back another step with her eyes suddenly very wide and staring. There was a rumble of thunder and a scatter of fat raindrops burst across the pavement.

"And yet,"—the Bhagavan lifted a hand, "you must not think I am deceiving you, Preeti. I stand before you as I truly am."

But Preeti backed another step, her heart thundering. He *had* to be more than he seemed. She had known it from the first. Oh, she *was* the unluckiest girl alive.

The raindrops drummed against the pavement and against the roof of the pavilion above them.

The Bhagavan Sanjit stepped forward as if to close the distance between them, but she backed again and lifted pressed-together hands to her forehead. "Namaste. I must go now," she managed to stammer.

"Preeti—"

"I *must* go now." She turned and went out into the rain at a jerky walk that became a stumbling run when she was sure he was out of sight. By the time she reached the room where she had eaten in the Rakshasa's presence, she was soaked. The heavy jewelled border of her sari slapped against her legs as she ran. Was it the rain that blinded her eyes, or was it tears? She flung past curtains, up the first stair, and through a door that looked familiar.

It was her own room. She pitched onto the bed and lay there with a hammering heart. What was he? A madman?

A god? Or—

You were made for love.

The only thing that was quite clear, even to her, was the impossibility of loving him. She thought her heart would break. Shiva Malhotra had only wanted her father's money. Babuji had protested, but he was willing in the end to let her bear his punishment as well as her own, because that was what a loving child did for her father. Only Sanjit told her—almost as if he meant it—that he would bear her pain for her...

She could not risk hoping. Amma Madhu's words came back to her.

Do not hope that the Bhagavan Sanjit will aid you. That flirt! Always, an eye for a pretty girl.... He makes sweet promises, and stirs up foolish hopes, and vanishes at the first sign of trouble.

"But the Rakshasa does everything he promises," Preeti breathed to herself, remembering Amma Madhu's next words.

"Everything..."

She fell asleep with the tears still on her face.

* * *

"Why? Why did you bring me here?"

It had been another interminable, wandering, echoing day in the palace of the Rakshasa, with no better company than her own dismal thoughts. So tonight, as she knelt at the dinner table across from the monster, the question broke out of her for the third time. And he had only asked how she had spent her day, and if all was to her liking.

The Rakshasa seemed displeased by her question.

"I have asked. I ask again. Marry me, Preeti."

"And if I say no?"

"Then you have said no."

"And if I say no tomorrow night?"

"Then you have said no tomorrow night."

"And the night after?"

"Also."

"How long am I to go on saying no?"

"Just as long as I please."

"How long will it be?" Under the table, Preeti clenched her hands into fists. "How long until you tire of asking? How long until you kill me?"

"Bus!" The word came out so quiet and low that it rattled the bowls on the table and every bone in Preeti's body. "Know this of me," he rumbled. "I do not tire. I do not lose patience. I wait as long as I have determined. But no longer."

Preeti ducked her head and murmured, "How much time do I have?"

"That I do not say. Bargain with yourself for time. But know that it is running out."

Preeti fidgeted with the border of her sari. "What shall I do in the meantime? The days are very long."

"You are provided with books and music."

"I cannot read."

He lifted a terrible claw. "That I can mend. Come here."

She flinched.

His eyes flamed at her. "I have promised you time," he said in the same low growl that hummed in her lungs. "Do you disbelieve me?"

"No. No, my lord." She stood and went shrinkingly toward him until she came within a pace or two of his throne, keeping her head bent so that she would not have to look at him so close, so terrible.

There always had been a stink about him, but suddenly she identified it as rotting flesh, the scent of death.

He lifted his clawed hand; she closed her eyes and managed, though a mad voice screamed in the back of her mind, to hold her ground while he laid it on her head.

She thought she heard him say a word, but it was in no tongue she knew. When his hand lifted she opened her eyes and glanced up at him.

To her astonishment, he was no more terrible at this close range than he had been far away. Or were his teeth less long and sharp, the red streaks above his eyes less angry?

Was there even a gleam of kindness in his eyes?

Whatever it was, it drew a tight answering smile from her, and for a moment she felt merely an uncomfortable intimacy, and not the terror that seemed to her, in its sudden absence, more fitting.

"Take up and read as you will," he said.

"Thank you." She retreated to her place at the table, and to the terror she had until now always felt for him. But she carried with her the memory of that odd uncomfortable closeness, and the world seemed awry, knocked a few degrees off its balance.

* * *

In the days that followed, the world tilted further.

Reading opened up to her a wide realm which until now she had perceived only dimly, at second-hand. The silence and solitude of the palace had once frightened her, but reading transmuted it into the most precious thing in that vast place, so that this new home of hers came by degrees to be less a terror than a sanctuary.

And although she could not bring herself to say anything but *no* when the nightly question came, Preeti found that the Rakshasa too could be borne with. Each night, before the question she dreaded, he also asked her what she had read. At first she had to compel herself to answer. These days she was almost eager for evening to come, so that she could ask him all the questions that rose in her mind.

One night she told him, "Today I read of a great city in the north, long ago, that used pipes to carry its water, and not slaves."

The Rakshasa nodded once. "I know the book. The water in this house is carried in the same way."

She thought of her bath water, always so clean, always

so pleasantly warm. "And there is also a fire to heat the water?"

"A hypocaust under the ground. Yes."

Preeti clasped her hands and leaned forward. "The book made this sound like a good thing. But it's no convenience to you, surely?" She knew by now that he had servants aplenty, if unseen. "Another servant to heat and carry the water would hardly impoverish you. It might even be cheaper than planning and building and maintaining such a system—"

"Perhaps," said the Rakshasa. "But ask the servants what they say."

"Well! Of course the servants would like the chance to lie about growing lazy and fat and considering themselves as good as their masters, but—"

The Rakshasa's eyebrows became more forbidding. "You speak of my only faithful people."

Preeti winced.

"In your father's house in the village Arora, you had no pipes to do your fetching and carrying. Would you have become fat and lazy without them?"

Preeti remembered the daily walks to the village well, the thankfulness she felt that they lived close enough to the river to bring their cow to the water rather than otherwise. And what if there had been pipes? The time was wanted for tilling and tending the garden, for stitching the new clothes she and her father so badly needed, even for reading…

"Is your servants' convenience so important to you?"

"Are they not men also? Are they not made for something better?"

But it was not the men who carried water. Preeti raised a disbelieving eyebrow. "Even the women?"

"Particularly the women."

"You are very kind to them," she said at last.

"So they tell me."

She bent her head and thought, *And me?* But she dared not say it.

"I will be kind to you, too, if you will allow it, Preeti."

Had he read her mind? "Allow it? –Oh, yes. Marry you."

"Will you?"

The rumble in his voice which, even in his gentlest moments, never entirely left him, reminded Preeti that one day it would be too late to say yes...

She hesitated.

The Rakshasa waited.

"No," she said at last, and looked up beseechingly. "Must you continue to ask?"

"Until the day I have chosen—yes."

His voice bristled again with warning, but Preeti felt heartened to persist. "Lord," she said, as gently as she could, "I tell you I will never bring myself to marry you. Please, must you continue to press me for an answer I cannot give?"

"Yes."

"I had rather die at once."

"Die?" he rumbled, and the red brows almost met. "Are you so weary of your life, when it is a gift I give you day by day?"

"It was a thing I *had*." A voice at the back of her mind told her that it was no good, that she should stop speaking while she had the chance, but she ignored it and plunged on. "I've always had my life. What puts it in your power, to give or take?"

"You come of the village Arora," said the Rakshasa. "Do you not?"

"Yes, but—"

"That place lies under sentence of death."

The words took her breath away for a moment. Then she faced up to him again. "Why? What have we done?"

"Rebellion. Those people are my servants. Those dwellings were built by my money, defended by my blade and my blood. Yet they slaughtered my servants and drove me out."

Preeti closed her eyes and saw the empty fort. The Demon Rajah. Amma Madhu, telling her to buy them peace a little longer. "I'm not one of them," she whispered. "I come from Cambay."

"You were born there," said the Rakshasa. "But your father was born in Arora."

"And you mean to punish me for a thing that my father's fathers once did?"

"No." He still spoke slowly, in the tone of one anxious to be understood. "No. If you are punished, it will be because ou share in that rebellion."

"But I don't!" He did not answer, and she tried to wallow the whine of protest in her voice. "Lord, truly, I don't."

He looked at her with calm and maddening disbelief. Her face warmed, but she did not dare to object again.

"I ask again," said the Rakshasa, "are you weary of your life? Is there anything more you desire?"

"Nothing," she muttered.

Again, that flat disbelief, as if he could see right into her mind.

And didn't she deserve a little happiness?

"Nothing, except... My father will be so lonely without me, my lord. Please, will you let me see him again? I want him to know I am alive and well."

A moment passed. Then the Rakshasa rose from his throne. "Ah! That is one request I cannot grant you."

"He is an old man." She jumped to her feet and followed him as he went to the door. "He has suffered so much bad luck. So much sorrow. I worry about him."

Under the door-lintel, the Rakshasa turned and towered over her, and his voice rattled her ribs. *"Bus.* I have said."

Preeti cringed back and the Rakshasa vanished behind the curtain. All the rest of that evening there was a sour taste in her mouth, as if she were guilty of some trespass upon the kindness of a friend. In vain she assured herself that *he* was the unreasonable one.

* * *

That night she saw the lord Sanjit again. Preeti heard his voice singing as she lay in her moonlit chamber:

"Listen to me, my love, and open to me! I have come from afar, the distance between us is gone! I'm here, I'm here!"

She did not remember rising, only going through the moonlight and looking out of a cloistered balcony to the garden below. He stood there on the path, singing, and every note of his voice wrenched at her heart.

"Look at me, my love, and have pity! I am drenched with dew and waiting at your door! I'm here, I'm here."

She blinked and he had gone. But then she turned and saw him coming through the cloisters to meet her, silvered by the moonlight. Her breath caught in her throat and she remembered why she so often thought him a god. He caught her around the waist and his breath brushed her cheek.

"Your hair is a cloud of rain, my love, and your feet I adore! You are altogether lovely."

Then he was gone again; she saw him passing by further down the passage, singing, *"I'm here, I'm here,"* and she went running after him in a floating turmoil of gauzy skirts.

Song burst from her own lips.

"I have unwound my veil, must I put it on again? I have washed my feet, must they go seeking you?"

"I'm here, I'm here." Only his voice lingered.

She caught a pillar in one of the endless rooms, catching

her breath, and her voice echoed through the palace. *"I opened to my love, but my love had already gone. O silent companions! Tell him, if you see him, that I am sick with love! Tell him I'm here, here, I'm here."*

And then she heard the call, soft and echoing, one more time. "I'm here."

Preeti woke with a jerk and sat up. Moonlight flooded her chamber through its many windows; it was like lying inside a pearl. Outside, trees sighed in the breeze. All the birds had fallen silent, and so, now, had the voice of the Bhagavan Sanjit.

Preeti jumped from her bed and fled to the window. Down in the garden, she saw him turning away and walking into the shadows.

No sound fell from her lips. Only her mouth formed his name, for the first time without any honorific.

"Sanjit…"

He could not have heard her. But he swung around, there on the borderland between light and shadow, and looked up at her with his lips parted a little and his eyes in shadow from the shock of dark hair that fell over his brow.

He lifted a hand and beckoned.

Preeti stared down at him for a moment longer, and then pulled herself away from the baluster and went with dragging steps back into her room, almost bent, as if struggling against some desert wind.

Let him not begin to sing again. Let him just go away.

If he sang, she would go running to him, and she dared not think what might happen if she did, if she listened to those words, sweet as honey.

Then she remembered the look on his face when she had come to the window, the yearning gesture of his hand. Might he not be sincere? After all, it took more than a common flirt to brave the wrath of the Rakshasa.

Unless...

The thought that had sent her backing away from him with sudden terror at their last meeting came back to her again. Had the Rakshasa laid a trap for her?

No. She knew him well enough by now to reject the thought out of hand. Traps were not in his nature. Inflexible adherence to his word—*that* was his nature. *That* was why he terrified her.

And he expected her to obey him, too. If he would not let her past the wall, if he would not even allow her to see her father, what would happen if he found her with Sanjit? He was a hard master. To go running out would sign her doom, and Sanjit's too, if they were found.

Preeti did not go to bed at once; instead she sat cross-legged on a couch and made tea, with plenty of warm milk, to calm herself. Then at last she slipped through the curtains of her bed and lay down. But it was no use. The moment she closed her eyes she could see Sanjit's face and hear his voice calling, *"I'm here, my love!"*

She flung up her hands and pressed them against her ears.

"You are altogether lovely!"

"Go away!" Suddenly, she was sitting up in bed. "Go away! Leave me! I can't love you! I *won't!*"

Her cry echoed away into the night and Preeti shivered, listening for some kind of reply. At first there was none. And then she heard it—the *crunch-crunch* of footsteps coming up the gravel path from the gate.

Sanjit! Preeti tumbled from the bed a second time and ran with outstretched arms through the billowing white curtains into the hall. She flew through that palace of pearl like a wind through a dozen silken doorways.

She came down a stair and out into the white courtyard, where the lotus-flowers slumbered on the bosom of the pool. She crossed the marble pavement and sprang up the steps that led to the portico of the palace to meet a shape rising up before her.

"Sanjit," she sobbed.

It come out into the moonlight and was the Rakshasa. And even at the dead of night, under the soft white light of the moon, the dark wet patches on his talons and teeth glistened red where the light struck them, and the sickly smell of fresh blood hung on the air…

Preeti stared at him for a moment. A scream rang in the air. Afterwards, she realised it must have been her own. Then it was as though a dark veil dropped between them. She did not even feel herself begin to fall.

* * *

Preeti woke with a gasp and found herself on her own bed. Had she dreamed that meeting in the courtyard? But then a whisper of sound caught her ear. She glanced over to the door and saw the curtain ripple like a waterfall and then continue its airy waving, as if it had just that moment been dropped behind a passer-by.

She fought through the hangings of her bed and the door curtains. The Rakshasa was still only a few steps down the passage, and he stopped and bent his head, but did not look at her, when he heard the faint groan of the curtain whisked aside.

Preeti breathed, "Turn. Turn and look at me."

The Rakshasa turned. A breeze came running down the passage toward her; it bore the scent of blood, and she was able to see the dark wetness on his muzzle and claws.

She stared at him a moment longer, and then turned from him toward the mirror at the end of the hall. There was blood on her white tunic and a smear on her forehead that was almost like the bridal sindoor. He must have carried her to her room when she fainted.

I have other fare.

She stared through the mirror into his flaming eyes. "Who?"

"One who earned my wrath."

Not Sanjit. Please, not Sanjit. *"Who?"*

"An evil man, a killer of men." He lifted a claw as if to gesture, then dropped it when she flinched. "My people may have driven me out, Preeti, but I still watch over them."

She kept staring into the mirror. "You ate a man. How could you?"

His voice deepened. "I have eaten men, women, children, and villages." He took a step forward, and Preeti whipped around to face him. "All my people lie under sentence of death. Tell me why I should spare them—or you."

Suddenly, the world that had seemed ever so slightly off-balance around her for the last few weeks turned completely upside down and Preeti dimly perceived a world in which she did not deserve anything, neither life nor luck. A world in which each day, no matter how dark or dreadful, came as an unexpected and delightful gift—

The injustice of that picture revolted her almost to nausea. She fell back a step with a wrenching gasp. How dare he? How *dare* he?

"I told you I do not share in their rebellion," she said. "Have you not seen that I have always tried to please you? What more could you ask?"

"One thing."

Again the world threatened to turn topsy-turvy, to a place where the gift of herself was no more than this creature's due. Where nothing she could do was able to please him because in withholding one thing, she withheld everything.

She uttered a fierce, jagged laugh that tore at her the whole way coming up, and spun back to the mirror with an outflung hand. "Look! *Look at yourself!* And then tell me, if you dare, that I should find it an easy thing to marry with *that*."

She stared at his reflection with wide and challenging eyes, and was amazed when he bent his head as if in silent acknowledgement of a fact. At that gesture, for some reason she did not trouble to investigate, her eyes were choked with tears. She put her hands up to her face and sobbed.

After a little while she took her hands away from her face and saw that he was still there.

"Do you love me?"

"You know the answer to that," he rumbled.

In the Rakshasa's tilted world, where it was a mercy to let her live, even for a day, the answer was *yes*.

"If you truly loved me, you would let me go."

"Not if it meant your destruction."

More tears rolled down her cheeks. "If you love me, why won't you show me in a way that I might understand?"

The Rakshasa stood there in the passage as still as granite, outlined against the billowing white of a curtain. "You have some way in mind."

"Let me go and see my father." Babuji…and Sanjit. "Just this once. For a few days."

He did not answer at once, and Preeti began to hope.

"I'll come back to you, I swear it. I'll come back and spend the rest of my life with you, without any complaint or murmur. I'll even try to love you. Only let me do this.

Not for myself, but for my father."

She turned from the mirror, pressing the palms of her hands together, and looked up at him with tears.

When he spoke at last, his voice was softer than she had ever heard it. "It will mean bad luck."

"My luck couldn't possibly be worse."

"For *me.*"

She dropped her hands to her sides. She should have known it was hopeless—

"Take this gem." Clumsily, for his sharp claws were made to clutch and tear, he held out to her a massive golden ring set with an emerald. "Lay it under your pillow when you sleep, and you will awake in your father's house."

Hope flickered into life within her.

"I give you a month. Put the ring under your head again when that time is over."

Moving as if in a dream, Preeti took the ring from him.

"But look at the stone often," said the Rakshasa. "Come back before the colour fades."

She clenched its smooth weight in her hand. "Why?"

He reached out one of his clawed hands with an oddly tender gesture. "Because, Preeti, although I cannot express it in many ways that you would understand, I do love you. And if you leave me too long alone, that love will kill me."

Preeti backed away from him, away from that granite shadow outlined against the blowing white curtain, so much afraid that he would change his mind that she did not remember to thank him until she stood on the threshold of her door. She pressed her palms together and bobbed her head once or twice. "Thank you. Thank you," she said, and darted away.

Chapter 3.

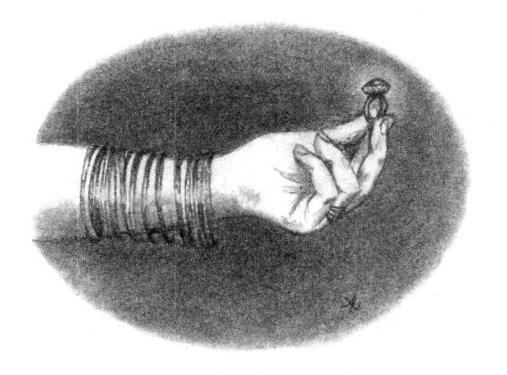

She woke the next morning, at once remembered the Rakshasa's promise, and bolted up in bed. When she did, Preeti's heart plummeted. From the richness of the room, she supposed that she must still be in the Rakshasa's palace. But then she heard bustle and movement outside, ran to the window and found herself looking out of one of the prosperous houses in the village Arora.

Her father's fortunes were restored! Not yet to the full tide, but a man like Om Nitin Kamla would have put the Rakshasa's gift of treasure to good work. In a little time, the great merchant's name might rise again.

Preeti leaned out the window. Down below in the square, a line of women waited to draw water at the well. Her eyes searched among them and among the men at their everlasting game of Nava Kankari before she realised she was looking for Sanjit. Surely he would come to her if he knew she was here. She would see him once without the Rakshasa threatening them, and say—but she did not know what she would say.

Beyond the square rose the wall of the empty fort, and from her vantage point she could see across it to the great keep beyond with black and staring windows. She remembered the Rakshasa saying, "My people have driven me out, Preeti, but I still watch over them."

The hairs prickled on the back of her neck. She turned away quickly, went back to her bed, and took out the Rakshasa's emerald ring from under the pillow. As a child she had hidden sweets and meaner trinkets in the hem of the bed-curtains; now, eager to run downstairs and find her father, she slid the ring in the same place.

By the bed was a chest she recognised from her room in the Rakshasa's palace. Preeti flung it open and robed and jewelled herself with hurrying fingers. Her anklets chimed to her quick steps going out of the room and down the stair to the atrium of the house.

There was a clang like a bell. Preeti looked across the room into the wide eyes and gaping mouth of her sister Radha. A cup rolled across the floor where it had fallen from nerveless fingers.

"Sister!" cried Preeti, holding out her hands.

"Preeti!" Radha gasped, looking more shocked than pleased. "We thought you were dead."

Preeti laughed. "Not yet."

Radha came smiling to her arms. "But look at you." She drew back, and stared Preeti up and down. "You're so *fine*. Did—did the creature give you all these?" Radha's fingers traced the gemmed ornament that lay on her hairline.

"All these," said Preeti with a bright smile. She did not add "And many more," for she felt vaguely aware that saying so would hurt her sister. "Radha, what about Babuji? Where—"

The smile fled Radha's face as if it had been wiped clean of expression. Preeti's fingers clenched tight on her sister's arms. "Radha, why have you come—"

"He's ill," said Radha in the breath of a whisper. "Oh, Preeti, he's very ill."

"Take me to him," she begged, and Radha led her to the portico that opened onto a courtyard full of shrubs and flowers. Her father was lying there on a couch, propped up on pillows with open eyes that stared unseeing into the distance.

On the edge of her vision, someone moved and for one wildly happy fraction of a moment blazing from the midst of her worry, she thought it was Sanjit. Then he walked into her vision and was only a portly old servant with a cup on a tray.

Preeti caught her step and backed under the door-lintel. "You go ahead," she murmured to her sister. "Break it to him gently."

Radha went to where Om Nitin Kamla lay like a dead man on the couch. She bent down, took the old merchant's hand, and murmured something into his ear. Her father's hand clenched more and more tightly on Radha's—and then his face turned toward Preeti and his other hand lifted.

Preeti gave a sob and ran forward, dropping to her knees, burying her face in her father's chest. He laid a hand on her head and stroked her hair. "My Preeti—my delightful lotus," he murmured. "Is it you? Have you really come back to me?"

Preeti lifted her head from the covers and laid her hand against his cheek. "Yes, Babu. But only for a short time. Only for a month. I have promised him I will return."

He gripped her hand. "Preeti—I should have stayed. I'll never forgive myself…"

"No, Babuji…"

"I am dying anyway," he rasped. "I let you take my place and I am broken—here." He touched his chest. "So it comes to the same thing in the end."

"No," said Preeti. "Look!"

Deliberately, she put out her two hands, waved them

over his head, and then pressed fisted knuckles to her temples.

"I took it upon me. I still take it upon me. The Rakshasa is not so unkind as you think. He has treated me well. I think that he even loves me in his own way. So much that he told me he'll die if I don't return in time." She smiled and wiped away tears. "So I'll tell you what I mean to do. Listen, Babuji! I'm going to nurse you. You're going to get well and strong again and become the richest merchant in Hindustan. Radha will give you fat grandchildren. And you'll live to a hundred and twenty."

"Why so long?" His voice creaked with effort, but there was a smile in his eyes, as though they once again played the make-believe games of her childhood.

"Because you have to live all the years that I can't, and have all the good luck that I might have had."

Radha frowned. "Luck doesn't work like that. Does it?"

"I don't know, Babuji," Preeti persisted, as if he had asked the question instead of her sister. "All I know is that I have given myself to the Rakshasa—or, well, I have given my life for yours, and I don't mean to be cheated. I want to know for the future that you are alive and well. Agreed?"

As she spoke, the smile faded out of his eyes. "Agreed." He sighed.

"Now sleep. I'll be here when you wake."

He nodded and closed his poor staring eyes. Preeti kissed his brow and went back inside with Radha, feeling the grief lying sour and heavy on her stomach despite her brave words.

Radha said, "It won't work, you know. He still feels guilty for letting you go. When you leave, he will go on dying."

Preeti sank onto a couch and buried her face in her hands. It wasn't supposed to be like this! Her sacrifice should have saved his life, not doomed it.

"If you stayed…" Radha began.

"I can't. *He* will be angry with me."

"So you lied. He doesn't love you."

Preeti looked up wonderingly. "I didn't lie. He really said that."

Radha lifted her own eyes to heaven and dropped to her knees in front of Preeti. "How do you know he was telling the truth?"

"He always tells the truth."

Radha gave a little hard laugh. "Then what's the difficulty? Stay here and wait for the demon to perish."

"I can't—" But then Preeti caught herself with a gasp as she realised how completely the Rakshasa had put himself in her power.

She tried to stop the thought there. "This very house is the Rakshasa's gift. He sent Babuji home with a load of treasure. Otherwise he would still be poor."

"But they say he's a man-eater, a menace to the whole countryside. And you can be free of him so easily. Just stay here and wait." Radha's eyebrows knitted together. "If we could only be *certain* when he was dead…"

And if the Rakshasa died, then she and Sanjit would be free...

Too late to stop herself now. "He gave me a jewel," Preeti murmured. "An emerald. So that if it begins to fade, I would know to return before it was too late."

"There!" Radha cried. "Nothing simpler!"

Preeti bit her lip, tempted. Then she shook her head. "I can't. What if he *doesn't* sicken? What if I make him angry and he comes after me?"

"Sister," Radha protested, "you're thinking only of yourself. Don't you have a responsibility to all these people? This monster has oppressed them for generations. All of them go in fear of him. And just think! It lies in your power to liberate them. So *very* easily."

It *would* be easy.

"Think of it," Radha said. "Think of the *injustice*. All his wealth. Who can tell how much richer this village would be, if not for him?"

Preeti glanced up and saw the twist of avarice in her sister's face. At the same moment the world tilted again and she saw her sister through the Rakshasa's eyes and almost recoiled.

"I'm not convinced he's so unjust. Or such a monster," she said in a harder voice, rising from her chair. "Besides, he trusted me."

She left Radha crestfallen in the atrium and went back up to her room. Sanjit was there. Not in the flesh, but his song hummed in her blood, and once she turned quickly, imagining a movement on the edge of sight, where she thought she saw him standing.

She had meant to go through her chest to see if the Rakshasa's silent servants had packed a book for her. But now she slammed down the lid, wrapped her head in the pallu of her sari, and went back down the stairs and out into the village square.

She pulled the rich fabric closer around her face, feeling out of place in that dusty glare. Once she had shrouded herself from view in shame for her bad luck. Now she shrouded herself from view in shame for her golden ornaments, her richly-wrought sari—

In shame for her good luck.

Preeti stopped halfway across the square and caught her breath. She let it out again in a soundless laugh. To these people, she had good luck.

Did they know she was a bride of the Rakshasa? If they knew it, would they still envy her? What if they knew her secret, that with each passing day it grew harder to pretend she did not see the handsome young Bhagavan Sanjit in every sudden movement, hear his voice in every unexpected word, turn to see him watching her in every dream?

That unless he could find a way to help her, she must soon part from him forever?

She gave herself a little mental shake and would have moved on, but a shadow fell across her feet. Preeti looked up into the eyes of the very woman she had come to find.

Amma Madhu stood before her with such a sharp smile lashing across her face that Preeti almost looked for blood in the corners.

"So you have returned. They always return, in the end."

Preeti stared back at her, and all at once a sour taste filled her mouth. *They always return, in the end.* She hadn't forgotten the Rakshasa's other brides. But she'd told herself she was special. She'd convinced herself that he really loved her. She'd even begun to hope she'd escape the fate of the others.

"What happens next?" she asked.

The midwife shrugged. "Weakness. Fever. Death. And ashes." The smile became a little sharper. "Look at your father."

Preeti stared back at her, and all the hopes she had begun to feel crumbled to the ground.

They were both going to die, weren't they?

Amma Madhu leaned in a little closer, and Preeti smelled bhang on her breath. "As I told you. The Rakshasa does everything he promises."

But he'd promised her she could see her father. That *he* would be the one to die if she stayed away too long.

Amma Madhu wheeled away, but Preeti reached out. "Stop."

The midwife turned.

"Have you seen the Bhagavan Sanjit? Is he here?"

Amma Madhu's eyes narrowed. "Perhaps."

"Will you take him a message for me?" Preeti unhooked

one golden earring and held it out.

Amma Madhu snatched at it and tucked the gold into her sari. "I cannot take any message. I do not know where the Bhagavan Sanjit is now, but I last saw him three days ago. He said he would return in a month."

* * *

She must stay, then, until Sanjit returned. As the days rolled by, Preeti busied herself in the house. Radha had the management of her father's money, and transacted business with passing caravans, to such profitable ends that Preeti left all their affairs in her hands. She herself passed the time sitting by her father's bedside with one of the several books she had found in her chest, reading aloud. Or she went into the kitchen, and cooked food to coax his appetite.

He was recovering. Gaining back a little strength, a little flesh, a little hope.

How much time had already gone by? Surely she could afford to stay a little longer. A few days, and her father would be strong enough to do without her. A few days, and Sanjit would return as he had promised Amma Madhu.

More than once she remembered the midwife's words about the brides that returned, sickened, and died. More than once she panicked when she felt something that might have been—but never was—a precursor to illness.

"How long have I been here, do you know?" she asked

Radha one evening as they sat over a late meal.

Radha, whose dealings with merchants required a stricter observance of time, shrugged. "Three weeks, maybe. You've a good few days left."

"Three weeks?" Preeti paused with a morsel of chapati halfway to her lips. "Are you sure?"

"Certainly no more," said Radha. "I know, because it was a day or two before you came that Pradip Gupta travelled by with a letter from my husband. He comes by each month about the same time."

Preeti told herself it might be wise to look at the emerald ring before she slept. But then it slipped her mind until the next morning while she was reading to her father in the portico.

Her voice faltered.

"What is it?" asked Om Nitin Kamla.

"I was thinking that I must go back to the Rakshasa soon."

He did not answer, but she felt the sudden anxiousness that struck him. "Stay a *little* longer, Preeti. Promise me."

"I will, Babuji, I will."

"Don't go before you've finished the book."

Preeti glanced at it. They would finish within the week, she was sure. "All right."

He smiled and immediately went to sleep. Preeti closed the book and went up to her room, where the window gave the best view of the village square. She opened the shutter and leaned over the sill.

Still no sign of the one she was waiting for.

"Sanjit will come in the end," she breathed to the evening light. "And then I'll know for certain that it has been a month."

Why must this time end? Why must the Rakshasa stand like a stone in the pathway of these serenely turning days? Could they not go on forever like this with luck and fortunes and health on the mend?

The thoughts blurred into sleep.

* * *

The sun bleeding on the rim of the sky warned Preeti that it was time for the evening meal. She pushed aside the white curtain of her room and went downstairs into the dining room with her fingers skimming the satin-smooth baluster of the stair. But tonight, unlike every other night, she found the room empty. The Rakshasa was not there.

At first Preeti thought he might not know she had returned. But then she saw a place laid for her at table and went out into the dusky garden with chiming steps, calling him.

Then she heard it, a groaning whisper dragging on the edge of hearing. "Preeti…"

With the sound, a formless fear took hold of her.

"My lord!" She turned and saw before her the pavilion by the pool where Sanjit had met her. In the dark, the lotus-flowers were blooming with a glare like firelight that lit up the heavy black bulk of the Rakshasa where he lay on the ground in the mud.

His head was turned toward her. One clawed hand was stretched out, as if reaching. She ran up to him and fell on her knees.

"You're dying," she breathed, and her skin turned cold as she realised that to her, it mattered.

A sound like the crack of a whip broke into the night. Preeti started up. There, a little way away, standing on the shore by the light of the lotus-blaze, her sister Radha clapped her hands.

There was a look of malicious triumph on her face.

"For gods' sakes, sister, have some respect!" Preeti cried, flinging up a hand to brush away her tears. When her wrist fell away, she thought for a moment that she stared back at herself out of Radha's eyes, saw the accusation and contempt on her own face, felt that triumph die down in her own heart—

She heard the Rakshasa's voice, weak and gasping, and the sound dragged her back into herself, where she knelt in the mud at his side. "I told you it was bad luck, Preeti—for me."

"Bad luck? No! No, it was *her*. *She* would have left you to die." Preeti reared up to point at her sister, but when she looked up it wasn't Radha. It was her own form, her own face that stared back at her with lips parted, appalled and guilty.

The world turned on its head.

* * *

She went from dream to waking on a surge of panic without any intermediate stage of drowsiness. The sun was up and cast fretted geometric patterns through the shutters of her room onto the floor and walls. Enough light to see by. More than enough light to find the little hard lump in the hem of her curtain that was the Rakshasa's ring.

It wasn't there.

Preeti stifled a sob and ran her hands along the whole lower hem of the curtain. Then the curtains on the other four sides of the bed. She looked under the bed. She flung her sheets and pillows about. Nothing. Not a sign of the gem.

She sat among the wreck of her covers and uttered a little high scream. It was more than a month. It *had* to have been more than a month. And she'd known it all along.

She heard his voice in the back of her mind: "All my people have risen against me and cast me out. All of them lie under sentence of death." She lifted her hands to her head with another strangled sob.

Something dreadful was happening, something she didn't understand. Why was everything working backward? Had not Amma Madhu told her that she would sicken with fever? Why then was the Rakshasa dying?

Where is that ring?

It had to have been more than a month. Amma Madhu had lied to her. Sanjit was never coming.

Sanjit *couldn't* come.

Preeti dressed, yanking on ghagra, choli, and dupatta with vicious and careless fingers, almost tearing the gauzy silks in her haste. At the foot of the stair she saw her sister sitting cross-legged at the breakfast table with a page of accounts. Preeti stormed across the floor in a whirl of silks, her fists clenched.

"Where is it?" she hissed. "Where is the Rakshasa's gem?"

Radha looked up. "Preeti? Aay! You look half-mad—"

"The emerald. Give it to me. I know you have it."

"I don't know what you're talking about." Radha scrambled to her feet and backed away.

"You're the only one I told," Preeti said. "You're the only one who would know where I hid it."

"Oh, Preeti," said Radha, rolling her eyes. "Don't tell me you were hiding things in your curtains again. I've told you a thousand times that the servants always find things there."

Preeti stared at her in sudden doubt. But Radha had always been a good liar.

She had also always hated any kind of physical discomfort.

"Sister," she said very quietly, "give me that ring before I pinch you black and blue."

"Oh, *deva*, Preeti, don't be such a madwoman. I was just

keeping it safe for you." Radha unhooked the slim gold chain she wore around her waist and pulled the ring up from where it was tucked into the waistline of her sari.

Preeti snatched it away with trembling hands. The stone was clear and colourless.

"Oh, no," she breathed, and then boiled into anger again. "All this time you've been *watching—!*"

"Why shouldn't I?" Radha challenged. *"You* haven't."

"No." The fire in Preeti's belly went out all of a sudden. "Alas!"

She turned away and came face to face with Om Nitin Kamla, leaning on a servant's arm.

"Babuji—"

"I heard."

She lifted the ring in a shaking hand. "See? There is still hope. Right in the centre—one green spark. I will go tonight."

He stared at the ring for a long time, as if unwilling to lift his eyes to her face. Finally he said in a low voice, "Must you?"

Was the world upside-down? Or did she stand upright for the very first time?

"Yes."

"He was going to kill you—"

"He might kill all of us. But he hasn't. And now, when I should be sick and dying, *he* is."

"Oh, I don't believe it." Radha was almost spitting in her fury. "Look at you! I wish I had *your* luck! You spend all your time eating and sleeping and putting on jewellery and taking off jewellery while the rest of us work our fingers to the bone! And now you think the Demon Rajah should come back and kill us all? Of course you do!"

Preeti whirled on her, white-lipped. Radha flinched, and at once, for some reason, Preeti was sorry for her. Sisters they might be, but Radha was incapable of understanding this mystery.

Preeti turned back to Om Nitin Kamla. "Come on, Babuji. Let's make the most of our last day."

* * *

When Preeti woke the following morning, she lay in her bed a few moments with her eyes screwed shut.

What would she do if she opened them to find herself still in her father's house? If the Rakshasa was dead?

Suddenly she heard the chirrup of a monkey and bolted up. The little black-faced creature sat on the sill of her window, watching with its head tilted.

"It worked," Preeti sobbed, and rolled from the bed.

Once she had spent hours every morning arranging hair and jewellery and painting her eyes with kohl before she felt properly armoured to meet the Rakshasa's glare. Today, she tumbled downstairs raking her fingers through her hair, still wearing yesterday's choli and ghagra.

She knew just where to go. Out into the garden, where the waterfall dived into the pool by the pavilion. "Lord!

Lord!" She burst through the white dining-room curtains onto the grass. The silence shattered under the bell strokes of her voice. "I'm here! I'm coming!"

Branches clawed and whipped her. Preeti threw up her arms to shield her face and stumbled out onto the pavement by the pool.

The Rakshasa was lying there. All in a pitiful heap, just as he had in her dream, with his face and one arm reaching toward her.

She stopped several paces away with her heart thundering. His eyes were closed, but she fancied there was something accusing in that outstretched arm. Moreover it was the first time she had ever seen the Rakshasa in sunlight, and in that harsh and unforgiving light he seemed even more ugly and forbidding.

"Lord," she cried. "Can you hear me?"

He didn't move. She caught her breath, but she couldn't hear his.

Tears blurred her vision. *"Haay tauba,"* she groaned, and flung herself foward, onto her knees, and threw her arms around the Rakshasa's neck, rank as it was with sweat. "Don't die. Don't die. I've come back to you. Please don't die!"

But the Rakshasa lay still and motionless, burning, burning...

In the back of her mind, Amma Madhu said, *"Weakness. Fever. Death. And ashes."*

Preeti gripped him more tightly. "Why? Why are you

doing this? It should have been me! This is *my* bad luck!"

Or not her bad luck. Her *fault*.

She kissed his terrible red-striped brow. The black fur on his face was the softest thing she'd ever touched. "Please," she begged. *"Please, Sanjit."*

The Rakshasa moved. Preeti pulled back a little, opened her eyes, and looked into the eyes of a young black-haired prince.

"Preeti," he groaned, and gripped her arms with trembling hands. "Preeti…" said the young lord Sanjit. "Say you'll marry me."

It was true. She stared at him with her mouth open in shock.

The sweat stood out on his pale forehead. He shuddered with effort. "Preeti, it's me."

God? Demon? What was he? A thousand questions stampeded through Preeti's mind. She ignored all of them. "Yes, I know. I… Sanjit, I can't marry you if you're dead."

He gave a sudden puff of laughter, but with the effort his grip on her arms slackened and he fell down on his elbow. "Then I must live." With one last effort he lifted his head again and smiled at her. Then he fell back to the ground, and Preeti hung over him, watching as sleep restored the flush of health to his wasted face.

* * *

The sun had set. It was time to eat.

Preeti knelt on the floor in her room. She was ready. She was washed, oiled, perfumed, draped, pleated, pinched, kohled, combed, and gemmed, but not excessively, because Sanjit preferred to see her face.

She was as nervous as a wild deer.

A tap came on the posts of her door.

"Come in," Preeti called.

It was the Rajah's major-domo, a very dark man in a snowy white turban and shirt. Hours ago he had come out with a litter to find them at the poolside, and had borne his master away to be washed and rested on a softer bed. And then, after an interminable space of time, he had brought word to Preeti to make ready, for the Rajah would eat with her.

Now he bowed to her with palms pressed together. "Rajakumari, my master asks if you will come to dine."

There was no more putting it off. Preeti rose from the floor, straightened the folds of her sari, looked once more into the mirror on the wall outside her door, and went down the stair as slowly as she dared.

Chink. Chink. He would know she was coming.

She went into the dining room with her eyes fixed on the ground.

Sanjit's voice was as deep and rich as it had been the first day he had spoken to her in the village. "Come. Sit."

She glanced up. He stood on the near side of the table, smiling, holding out his hand. Preeti went to him and would have touched his feet, but he caught her by the shoulders.

"No, Preeti."

She still kept her eyes on the floor. "Lord, I know that you love me now. Can you forgive me for doubting?"

His finger lifted her chin and she looked into tender eyes. "You were made for forgiveness."

"But you appeared so terrible."

"To my enemies, I *am* terrible."

"Your enemies." She put a hand on his arm. "Radha and Amma Madhu, and even Babuji...all of them think you're a monster. Will they never know?"

"That I do not say." But his smile put heart into her.

For she too had been his enemy. "I don't understand," she said after a moment. *"I* should have sickened. *I* should have died, just like the others. How was I different?"

He laughed. "But don't you remember, O lovely one? *I* took your bad luck."

S.D.G.

About the Author

Suzannah Rowntree lives in a big house in rural Australia with her awesome parents and siblings, reading academic histories of the Crusades and writing historical fantasy fiction that blends folklore and myth with historical fact. She is the author of the historical fantasy series Watchers of Outremer as well as the Arthurian fantasy Pendragon's Heir and a series of fairytale retellings.

You can connect with me on:
- https://suzannahrowntree.site
- https://twitter.com/suzannahtweets

Subscribe to my newsletter:
- https://www.subscribepage.com/srauthor

Also by Suzannah Rowntree

The Fairy Tale Retold Series
 The Rakshasa's Bride
 The Prince of Fishes
 The Bells of Paradise
 Death Be Not Proud
 Ten Thousand Thorns
 The City Beyond the Glass

The Pendragon's Heir Trilogy
 The Door to Camelot
 The Quest for Carbonek
 The Heir of Logres

The Watchers of Outremer Series
 Children of the Desolate
 A Wind from the Wilderness
 The Lady of Kingdoms

More Fairy Tales...

The Prince of Fishes
Not all wishes should be granted... Will Michael and Eudokia's ambition destroy an empire?

The Bells of Paradise
Never eat the faerie fruit... but when Janet does just that, it's up to John to face Faerie to save her.

Death Be Not Proud
Ruby Black is the spitting image of a dead girl. Is it going to get her killed?

Ten Thousand Thorns
What if Sleeping Beauty was a martial artist? Could her sword skill defeat the evil emperor?

The City Beyond the Glass
What if the Twelve Dancing Princesses tried to steal your soul? Gemma has only one chance to escape the Glass Doge...

Printed in Great Britain
by Amazon